Enid

A FARAWAY TREE
ADVENTURE

The
Land of
TOYS

For Anna
A. P.

HODDER CHILDREN'S BOOKS
Text first published in Great Britain as chapters 13-15 of *The Magic Faraway Tree* in 1943
First published as *A Faraway Tree Adventure: The Land of Toys* in 2017
by Egmont UK Limited
This edition published in 2021 by Hodder & Stoughton Limited

3 5 7 9 10 8 6 4 2

The Magic Faraway Tree ®, Enid Blyton ® and Enid Blyton's signature are registered
trade marks of Hodder & Stoughton Limited
Text © Hodder & Stoughton Limited
Cover and interior illustrations by Alex Paterson © Hodder & Stoughton Limited

A CIP catalogue record for this book is available from the British Library.

ISBN 978 1 444 95990 1

Printed and bound in China

The paper and board used in this book are made from wood from responsible sources.

Hodder Children's Books
An imprint of
Hachette Children's Group
Part of Hodder & Stoughton
Carmelite House
50 Victoria Embankment
London EC4Y 0DZ

An Hachette UK Company
www.hachette.co.uk
www.hachettechildrens.co.uk

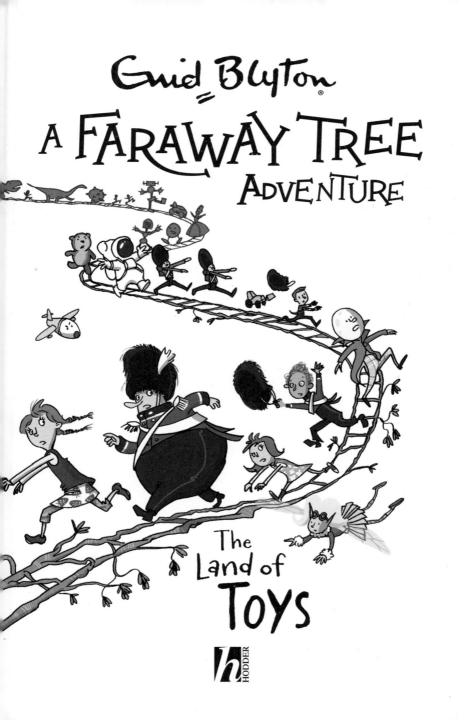

Enid Blyton

A FARAWAY TREE
ADVENTURE

The Land of Toys

h HODDER

The World of the FARAWAY TREE

MOON-FACE lives at the very top. In his house is the start of the **SLIPPERY-SLIP**, a huge slide that curves all the way down inside the trunk of the tree.

SILKY lives below Moon-Face. She is the prettiest little fairy you ever did see.

SAUCEPAN MAN is a funny old thing. His saucepans make lots of noise when they jangle together, so he can't hear very well.

CHAPTER ONE
Silky's News

One afternoon Silky came to see the children as they were all **working hard in the garden**. She leaned over the gate and called to them.

'Hello! I've come to **tell you something!**'

'Oh, hello Silky!' cried everyone. 'Come in. We can't stop work because we've got to finish clearing this patch before dinner.'

Silky came in. She sat down on a bench. 'The **Old Saucepan Man** wants to give a party,' she said. 'And he says, will you come?'

'Is it his birthday?' asked Joe.

'Oh, no. He doesn't know when his birthday is,' said Silky. 'He says he hasn't got one. This is just a party. You see, the **Land of Goodies**

is coming soon, and Saucepan thought it would be a good idea to go there with a large basket and collect as many good things to eat as he can find, and then **give a party** in Moon-Face's room, so we can eat all the lovely things.'

'That sounds great!' said Rick, who loved eating good things. 'When shall we come?'

'Tomorrow,' said Silky. 'About three o'clock. Will that be all right?'

'Oh, yes,' said Beth. 'Mother says we've been very good this week, so she's sure to let us come to the Saucepan Man's party tomorrow. We'll be there! When is Saucepan going to get the **goodies?**'

'Tomorrow morning,' said Silky. 'He says that the Land of Goodies will be there then. Well, goodbye. I won't stay and talk today, as I said I'd make some **Pop Cakes** and **Google Buns** for tomorrow as well. I might make some **Toffee Shocks**, too.'

Silky went. The children talked excitedly about the party.

'I hope there will be Danish pastries,' said
Rick.

'Danish pastries! At a party!' said Beth.

'Well, why not?' said Rick. '**They're**
delicious. I hope there will be pink and
yellow ice-cream too.'

Everyone felt excited when the next
afternoon came. Mother said they could go,
but she wouldn't let them wear their best
clothes. 'Not if you're going to climb trees,'
she said. 'And, Rick, please don't get your
clothes wet this time. If you do, you'll have to
stay in all day while I dry them.'

The children ran to the **Enchanted Wood**.
They had to climb up the tree the ordinary
way, because there was no rope that day.
Up they went, shouting a greeting
to the Owl in his room, to the
Angry Pixie and to Dame Washalot.

They reached Moon-Face's house. He and
Silky were setting out cups and saucers
and plates ready for **all the goodies** that
Saucepan was going to bring back. Silky
passed a bag around. 'Have a Toffee Shock?'
she said.

All the children except Rick had had Toffee Shocks before, and, as long as you knew what the toffee did, it was all right. But if you didn't, it was **a bit alarming**.

A Toffee Shock gets bigger and bigger and bigger as you suck it, instead of smaller and smaller – and when it is so big that there's no more room for it in your mouth, it suddenly **explodes** – and goes to nothing. Joe, Beth and Frannie watched Rick as he sucked his Toffee Shock, nudging one another and giggling.

Rick took a big Toffee Shock, as he was rather a greedy boy. He popped it into his mouth and sucked hard. It tasted delicious. But it seemed to get **bigger** and **bigger**.

Rick tried to tell the others this, because it surprised him. But the Toffee Shock was now so big that he could hardly talk.

'**Oooble, ooble, ooble!**' he said.

'What language are you talking, Rick?'

asked Moon-Face, with a giggle.

Rick looked really alarmed. His toffee was now so enormous that he could hardly find room in his mouth for it. And then suddenly it **exploded** – and his mouth was empty!

'Oooh!' said Rick, opening and shutting his mouth like a goldfish. 'Oooh!'

'Don't you like your toffee?' said Silky, trying not to giggle. 'Well, spit it out if you like, and have something else.'

'It's gone!' said Rick. Then he saw the others laughing, and he guessed that Toffee Shocks were not the usual kind of toffee. He began to laugh, too. **'Gosh, that did frighten me!'** he said. 'I'd love to give my old school teacher a Toffee Shock!'

CHAPTER TWO
The Land of Toys

Moon-Face looked at his clock. 'Old Saucepan is a long time,' he said. 'It's half past three now, and he promised to be back really quick.'

'Hello – there's somebody coming now,' said Moon-Face, **as he heard footsteps on the ladder that led up through the cloud**. 'Perhaps it's old Saucepan. But I can't hear his kettles clanking.'

Down the ladder came a wooden soldier, wearing the red uniform of a guard, with a black helmet. He saluted as he went past.

'Hey!' shouted Moon-Face suddenly. 'Wait a minute! How is it that you live in the Land of Goodies?'

'I don't,' said the wooden soldier, in surprise.

'I live in the Land of Toys.'

'What! Is the Land of Toys up there now?' cried Moon-Face, standing up in amazement.

'Of course!' said the soldier. 'The Land of Goodies **doesn't arrive until next week**.'

'Oh,' groaned Moon-Face, as the soldier disappeared down the tree. 'Old Saucepan has made a mistake. He's gone to the Land of Toys instead of to the Land of Goodies. I expect he is hunting everywhere for nice things to bring down to us – **he's such an old silly** that he wouldn't know it wasn't the right land.'

'We'd better go and tell him,' said Silky. 'You children can stay here till we come back, and then **we'll have a nice feast of Pop Cakes and Google Buns**. Help yourself to Toffee Shocks while we're gone.'

'We'll come too,' said Beth, jumping up. 'The Land of Toys sounds exciting. I wish I'd brought my doll. She would have loved to visit the Land of Toys.'

'Is it a dangerous land?' said Joe. 'Or just toys come to life?'

'Of course it's not dangerous,' said Silky.

They all went **up the ladder**. They were
very anxious to see what the Land of Toys
was like. It was exactly how they imagined
it would be!

CHAPTER THREE
Saucepan Gets into Trouble

Dolls' houses, toy shops, toy stations stood about everywhere, but much **bigger** than real toys. Teddy bears, dolls of all kinds, stuffed animals and clockwork toys ran or walked about, talking and laughing.

20

'**Wow! This is fun!**' said Beth. 'Oh, look at those wooden soldiers all walking in a row!'

They were just like the soldier who had come down the ladder at the top of the tree.

The children stared round, but Moon-Face beckoned them on.

'Come on,' he said. 'We've got to find out where the Old Saucepan Man has got to! I can't see him anywhere.'

The six of them wandered about the Land of Toys. Clockwork animals ran everywhere. A big Noah's Ark suddenly opened its lid and let out lots of wooden animals walking in twos. Noah came behind, singing. The Saucepan Man was nowhere to be seen.

'I'd better ask someone if they've seen him,' said Moon-Face at last. **So he stopped a big teddy bear** and spoke to him.

'Have you seen a little man covered with kettles and saucepans?' he asked.

'Yes,' said the teddy bear at once. 'He's naughty. He tried to steal some toffee out of the shop over there.'

'I'm sure Saucepan wouldn't steal a thing!' said Joe angrily.

'Well, he did,' said the teddy bear. 'I saw him.'

'I know what happened,' said Moon-Face, suddenly. 'Old Saucepan thought this was the Land of Goodies. He didn't know it was the Land of Toys. So when he saw the shop he thought he could take as many things as he liked. You can in the Land of Goodies, you know. And people must have thought he was stealing.'

'Oh, dear,' said Silky, in dismay. 'Teddy Bear, what happened to the Saucepan Man?'

'The policeman came up and took him off to jail,' said the teddy bear. 'There's the policeman over there. **You can ask him all about it**.'

The teddy bear went off. The children,
Moon-Face and Silky went over to the
policeman. He told them it was quite true
what the teddy bear had said – Saucepan had
tried to take toffee out of the shop, and he
had been locked up.

'Oh, **we must rescue him!**' cried Joe at
once. 'Where is he?'

'You must certainly not rescue him,' said
the policeman, angrily. 'I shan't tell you
where he is!'

And no matter how much the children begged him, he would NOT tell them where he had put **poor Saucepan**.

'Well, we must just go and look for him ourselves, that's all,' said Joe. And the six of them wandered off through the Land of Toys, calling loudly as they went.

'Saucepan! **Dear old Saucepan!** Where are you?'

CHAPTER FOUR
A Silly Song

The children, Moon-Face and Silky went down the crooked streets of the Land of Toys, calling the Old Saucepan Man.

'Of course, Saucepan can't hear very well,' said Joe. 'He might not hear us calling him, even if he was locked up somewhere near by.'

They went on again, **shouting and calling**.

The toys hurrying by stared at them in surprise.

'Why do you keep calling "**Saucepan, Saucepan**"?' asked a well-dressed doll. 'Are you selling saucepans, or something?'

'No,' said Joe. 'We're looking for a friend.'

Just then Silky heard something. She clutched Joe's arm. 'Sh!' she said. '**Listen!**'

Everyone stood still and listened. Then,
floating on the air came a well-known voice,
singing a silly song:

'Two trees in a teapot,

Two spoons in a pie,

Two clocks up the chimney.

Hi-tiddley-hie!'

'It's Saucepan!' cried Joe. 'Nobody but Saucepan sings those silly songs. Where is he?'

They looked all round. There was a toy soldier fort not far off, but, of course, much bigger than an actual toy fort would be. The song seemed to come from there.

'Two mice on a lamp-post,

Two hums in a bee,

Two shoes on a rabbit.

Hi-tiddley-hee!'

Joe laughed loudly. 'I never knew such a stupid song,' he said. 'I can't imagine how old Saucepan can make it up. It's coming from that fort. That's where he is locked up.'

Everyone looked at the red-painted fort. Soldiers walked up and down it. A drawbridge was pulled up so that no one could go in or out. When a soldier wanted to go out the drawbridge was let down and the soldier stepped over it. Then it was pulled up again.

'Well, Saucepan is definitely in there,' said Moon-Face. 'And, by the way, don't call to him, any of you. We don't want the soldier guards to know that there are any friends of his here – or else they will guess that we want to rescue him.'

'Oh, **do let's try** and let him know we're here,' said Beth. 'He'd be very glad as he must feel so worried and unhappy.'

'I know a way of telling him we are here, without anyone guessing we are friends of his,' said Joe suddenly. 'Listen.'

He stood and thought for a moment. Then he raised his voice and sang a little song:

'Two boys in the high road,

Two girls in the street,

Two friends feeling sorry.

Tweet-tweet-tweet-tweet-tweet!'

Everyone roared with laughter. 'It's very clever, Joe,' said Rick. 'Two boys – Saucepan

will know that's you and me – two girls – that's Beth and Frannie – two friends, Silky and Moon-Face! Saucepan will know we're all here!'

A terrible noise came from the fort – a **clanging and a banging, a clanking and crashing**. Everyone listened.

'That's old Saucepan dancing round to let us know he heard and understood,' said Joe. 'Now the thing is – how are we going to rescue him?'

36

They walked down the street, talking, trying to think of some good way to save poor Saucepan. They came to a clothes shop. In it were dolls' clothes of all sorts. In the window was a set of sailor's clothes, too. Joe stared at them.

'Now, **I wonder**,' he said. 'I just wonder if they've got any soldier's clothes. Moon-Face, lend me your money bag if it's got any money in it.'

Moon-Face put his money bag in Joe's hand. Joe disappeared into the shop. He came out with three sets of bright red soldier guard's uniforms, with big, black helmets.

'**Come on**,' he said in excitement. 'Come somewhere where we shan't be seen.'

They all hurried down the street and came to a field where **some toy cows stood grazing**.

They climbed over the gate and went behind the bushes. 'Rick, see if this uniform will fit you,' said Joe. 'I'll put this one on.'

39

'But Joe – Joe – what are you going to do?' asked Beth in surprise.

'I thought you would have guessed,' said Joe, putting the uniform on quickly. 'We're going to see if we can **march into the fort** and get old Saucepan out! I should think they will let down the drawbridge for us if we are dressed like the other soldiers.'

'Is this third suit for me?' asked Moon-Face.

'**No, Moon-Face**,' said Joe. 'I didn't think you'd look a bit like a soldier, even if you were dressed like one. You must stay outside and look after Beth, Frannie and Silky. This third suit is for old Saucepan. The soldiers won't let us take him out of the fort covered in kettles and saucepans! They will know it's the prisoner and will stop him. He'll have to take off his kettles and things and wear this uniform. Then, maybe we can rescue him easily.'

'**Joe, you really are very clever**,' said Silky.

Joe felt very pleased. He buckled his belt, and put on his black helmet. He did look impressive! So did Rick.

'**Now we're ready**,' said Joe. 'Moon-Face, if by any chance Rick and I are caught, you must take the girls safely back to the tree. OK?'

'OK,' said Moon-Face. 'Good luck, boys!'

CHAPTER FIVE
An Exciting Rescue

Everyone went out of the field and walked back to the fort. When they got near it, Rick and Joe began to march very well indeed. **Left, right, left, right, left, right!**

They came to the fort. '**Soldier, let down the drawbridge!**' yelled Joe, in his loudest and most commanding voice.

The guard peered over the wall of the fort. When he saw the two well-dressed soldiers, he saluted at once, and began to let down the drawbridge.

Crash! It fell flat to the ground, and Rick and Joe walked over it into the fort.

Creak, creeee-eak! The drawbridge was drawn up again. Joe and Rick marched right into the fort. Soldiers saluted at once.

'I wish to talk to the prisoner here,' said Joe.

'**Yes, sir**,' said a wooden soldier, saluting. He took a key from his belt and gave it to Joe. 'First door on the right, sir,' he said. 'Be careful. He might be dangerous.'

'Thanks. Good man,' said Joe, and marched to the first door on the right. He unlocked it and he and Rick went in and shut the door. Saucepan was there! When he saw the two soldiers, he fell on his knees.

'Set me free, set me free!' he begged. 'I didn't mean to steal the toffee. I thought this was the Land of Goodies.'

'Saucepan! It's us!' whispered Joe, taking off his helmet so that Saucepan could see

him plainly. 'We've come to save you. Put on
this uniform, quick!'

'But **what about my kettles and
saucepans?**' said Saucepan. 'I can't leave
them behind.'

'Don't be silly. You'll have to,' said Joe.
'**Quick, Rick**, help him off with them.'

The two boys stripped off every pan and made Saucepan dress up in the red uniform. He trembled so much with excitement that they had to do up every button for him.

'Now march close to us and don't say a word,' said Joe, when Saucepan was ready. His kettles and saucepans lay in a heap on the floor. He fell over them as he scrambled across to Joe and Rick. Joe opened the door. All three marched out, keeping in step. **Left, right, left, right, left, right!**

The other soldiers in the fort looked up but saw nothing but three of their comrades – or so they thought. Joe shouted to the guard:

'Let down the drawbridge!'

'Very good, sir!' cried the guard, and let it down with a crash. Joe, Rick and Saucepan marched out at once. **Left, right, left, right, left, right.**

Moon-Face and the girls could hardly
believe that the third soldier was old
Saucepan. He did look different in his
uniform, without his pans hung all round him.
Silky flew to hug him.

And then the guard of the fort yelled out
in a loud voice: 'I believe that's the prisoner! I
believe he's escaped! **Hey, after them!**'

'**Quick! Run! Run!**' cried Joe. And they all ran. **Fast!** Soldiers poured out of the fort after them, teddy bears and dolls joined in the chase, and animals pattered behind on four feet.

52

'**To the hole in the cloud!**' shouted Joe.
'Run, Beth; run, Frannie! Oh, I hope we get
there in time!'

CHAPTER SIX
A Shock for the Toys

How the children and the others ran! They knew well that if they were caught they would be put into the toy fort – and then the Land of Toys would move away from the Faraway Tree, and goodness knows how long they might have to stay there!

So they ran at top speed. Frannie fell behind a little, and Joe took her hand to help her along. **Panting and puffing**, they raced down the streets of the Land of Toys, trying to remember where the hole was that led down through the cloud to the Faraway Tree.

Joe remembered the way. He led them all
to the hole – and there was the ladder, **thank
goodness**!

'Down you go!' cried Joe to Silky, Beth and
Frannie. 'Hurry! Get into Moon-Face's room
quickly.'

Down the girls went, and then Rick, Moon-
Face, Saucepan and Joe. Joe only just got down
in time, because a big teddy bear had almost
caught them up – and as Joe went down he
reached out and tried to catch Joe's shirt.

Joe jerked himself away. His shirt tore — and he half slid, half climbed down the ladder to safety. Soon he was in Moon-Face's house with the others — **but what was this?** The toys did not stay up in their land — they poured down the ladder after the children and their friends!

'They're coming in here!' yelled Moon-Face. 'Oh, why didn't we shut the door?'

But it was too late then to shut the door.
Wooden soldiers, teddy bears and dolls poured
into Moon-Face's funny round room – and
Moon-Face, **quick as a flash**, pushed them
all towards the middle of his room.

The opening of the **slippery-slip** was
there – and one by one all the surprised toys
fell into the hole and found themselves sliding
wildly down the inside of the tree!

As soon as Joe and the others saw what Moon-Face was doing, they did the same.

'**Down you go!**' said Joe to a big teddy bear, giving him a good push – and down he went.

'A push for you!' yelled Rick to a big rag doll – and down the slide went the doll.

Soon the children could do no more pushing, because **they began to giggle**. It was so funny to see the toys rushing in, then being pushed down the slide, shrieking

and kicking. But after a while no more
toys came, and Moon-Face shut his door.
He **flung himself** on his curved bed, and
laughed till the tears ran down his cheeks.

   'What will the
toys do?' asked Joe at last.
   'Climb back up the tree to the Land of
Toys,' said Moon-Face, drying his eyes. 'We'll
see them out of my window. They won't cause
us **any more trouble!**'

After about an
hour the toys began
to come past Moon-
Face's window, slowly,
as if they were tired. Not
one of them tried to open the

door and get into Moon-Face's house.

'They're afraid that if they don't get back
into their land at once, it will move away!'
said Silky. 'Let's sit here and watch them all –
and have a few Google Buns and Pop Cakes.'

'I'm so sorry to have caused all this trouble,'
said the Saucepan Man. 'And I didn't bring
anything back to eat either. You see, I really
thought, when I got into the **Land of Toys**,
that it was the **Land of Goodies**, because one
of the first things I saw was that shop selling
toffee. And in the Land of Goodies you can

just take anything you like without paying for it – so of course I went right into the shop and began to empty some toffees out of a box. That's why they put me into jail. **It was dreadful**. Oh, I was glad to hear Joe singing. I knew at once that you would try to rescue me.'

This was a very long speech for Saucepan to make. He looked so unhappy and sorry that everyone forgave him for making such a silly mistake.

'Cheer up, Saucepan,' said Moon-Face. 'The Land of Goodies will soon come along – and we'll ALL go and visit it, not just you – and we'll have **the biggest feast we have ever had**.'

'Oh, but do you think we should?' began Joe. 'Honestly, we seem to **get into a fix every time we go up the ladder.'**

'I'll make quite sure that the Land of Goodies is there,' said Moon-Face. 'Nothing can go wrong if we visit it. Don't be afraid. I must say, Joe, you and Rick and Saucepan **look very grand** in your soldier's uniforms. Are you always going to wear them?'

'Oh – I forgot we haven't got our proper clothes,' said Joe. 'Mother will be cross if we leave them in the Land of Toys.

We left them under a bush near the fort.'

'And I left **my lovely kettles and saucepans** in the fort,' said Saucepan in a sad voice. 'I feel funny without them. I don't like being a soldier. **I want to be a Saucepan Man**.'

'I'd like you to be our dear old Saucepan Man, too,' said Silky. 'It doesn't seem you, somehow, dressed like that. But I don't see how we are going to get anything back. Surely none of us is going back into the Land of Toys again!'

Just then three sailor dolls, last of all the toys, came climbing slowly up the tree. They were crying. Their sailor clothes were torn and soaking wet.

Moon-Face opened his door. 'What's the matter?' he asked. 'What's happened to you?'

'Awful things,' said the first sailor. 'We were climbing up the tree when we came to a window, and we all peeped in. And **a very angry pixie** flew out at us and pushed us off the branch. The Faraway Tree was growing thorns just there and they tore our clothes to bits. And then a whole lot of washing water came pouring down the tree on top of us and soaked us. So we feel dreadful. **If only** we could get some new clothes!'

'**Listen!**' cried Joe suddenly. 'How would you like to have our soldier uniforms? They are quite new and very good.'

'**Oooh!**' said all the sailor dolls together. 'We'd love that. Would you really give us those? We'll get into trouble if we go back to the Land of Toys like this.'

'We'll give you them on one condition, sailor dolls,' said Joe. 'You must find our own things in the Land of Toys and throw them down the ladder to us. We'll tell you where they are.'

'We can easily do that,' promised the sailors. So Joe, Rick and Saucepan stripped off their **lovely uniforms** and gave them to the sailor dolls who took off their torn blue clothes and dressed themselves in the red trousers, tunics and helmets. They looked very nice.

'Now, you will find our clothes for us, won't you?' said Joe. '**We are trusting you, you see**.'

'We are very trustworthy,' said the dolls, and ran up the ladder after Joe had told them exactly where to find everything.

Joe, Rick and Saucepan sat in their underwear and **shivered** a little, because the uniforms had been warm.

'We'll look funny going home like this if those sailors don't keep their word!' said Rick. '**As a matter of fact**, I'd have liked to keep that uniform. I like it much better than my clothes.'

CHAPTER SEVEN
Back to Normal

'**Look –
something's
coming down
the ladder!**' cried
Moon-Face, and
they all ran out to
see. 'How quick the
sailor dolls have been
– or soldier dolls, as
I suppose we should
call them now.'

Two sets of clothes
tumbled down
the ladder and the
children caught them.

Then came a **clatter and clanging** as kettles and saucepans came down too. Saucepan was delighted. He put on a pair of ragged trousers and a **funny old coat** that came down with the pans – and then Silky helped him to string his kettles and saucepans round him as usual. 'Now you look like our dear old Saucepan again,' said Silky. The boys dressed too. Then Joe looked at Moon-Face's clock.

'We must go,' he said. 'Thanks for the Pop Cakes and everything. Now, Saucepan, **don't get into any more trouble** for a little while!'

'Smile?' said Saucepan, mishearing again. 'I am smiling. Look!'

'That's a grin, not a smile!' said Joe, as he saw Saucepan smiling from ear to ear. 'Now don't get into any more **TROUBLE!**'

'Bubble? Where's a bubble?' said Saucepan, looking all round. 'I didn't see anyone blowing bubbles.'

The children grinned. Saucepan was always very funny when he heard things wrong. 'Come on,' said Beth. 'Mother will be cross if we're home too late. Goodbye, Moon-Face. Goodbye, Silky. We'll see you again soon.'

'Well, don't forget to come to the Land of Goodies with us,' said Silky. 'That really will be fun. Nearly as much fun as the **Land of Do-As-You-Please**.'

'We'll come,' promised Beth. 'Don't go without us. Can I have a red cushion, Moon-Face? Thank you!'

One by one the four children **slid** swiftly down the **slippery-slip** to the bottom of the tree. They shot out of the trapdoor, gave the red squirrel the cushions and set off home.